The Santamobile

Moses Solomon

The *Santamobile*
© 2012 by Alexander F. Lee

cover illustration by Elizabeth Babicz
© 2012 by Alexander F. Lee
All Rights Reserved

ISBN 978-0-9894902-0-7
eISBN 978-1-301-52534-8

Printed in the United States of America

For My Wife,
With All My Love

My sincere thanks go to my editor, Suzy Vitello, who pushed me for greater character depth, and to Elizabeth Babicz, for her wonderful artwork.

1. The Return of Santa Claus

Scooter, diminutive among the other elves and far younger, squinted over the tops of the evergreen forest at the billowing, angry clouds rolling in from the southeastern sky. The faint whisper of a frosty breeze ruffled the highest of the overhead branches. The crowd of about a hundred fur-clad elves and uncounted forest animals that milled about the expansive clearing stayed quiet. It was almost midnight of the 25th, a full twenty-four hours since the team had departed for their annual sojourn around the world, following the time zones as the earth rotated below them.

There hadn't been a year like this one in a long time. Scooter thought back to his childhood, and the year of the Great Blizzard. That historic storm had been an anomaly. Scooter wasn't sure if this year's was or not. Like everyone else in the elf community, he kept abreast of the current news by picking up the available satellite broadcasts. According to most of the latest scientific publications, the earth was warming and changing, the atmosphere growing more temperamental and tempestuous. The worldwide weather forecast this Christmas Eve had been for violent pockets of turbulence and an abundance of storm systems throughout the northern hemisphere. Scooter couldn't help but dwell on how Santa would fare, under these conditions.

The roar of a motor interrupted his thoughts. A snowmobile emerged from behind a grove of evergreens, snow kicking up in its wake as it descended the knoll. Inside, the Chief of Staff, the imposing (for an elf) Piotr, and the chief mechanic and Scooter's team leader, Serge, accompanied a bundled-up Mrs. Claus.

Scooter smiled at the sight of Mrs. Claus. Right on time, as usual, her appearance signaled that their long wait was almost over.

Serge drove the snowmobile into the taxi area and brought it to a stop amidst the elves. Piotr helped Mrs. Claus, clutching her thick thermal muffler while still sipping her large tea mug, step out onto the snow. Questions immediately peppered her from all directions.

"What's the latest weather report, Mrs. Claus?"
"Should we prepare blankets?"
"Do you think Santa got airsick?"
Mrs. Claus released her muffler and raised her

free hand. "I only know..." Her steady, clear voice calmed the murmur. "...that Santa always appreciates a refill for his cider mug, upon landing." She gave everyone a warm, gracious smile. "I'm sure he'll have plenty of stories for us about this year's trip."

Scooter smiled. He never grew tired of Santa's stories of the many children of the world. Though they were surrounded by the technical advancements of the modern world, there was something timeless and magical about Santa and Mrs. Claus. Having been born and raised here at the North Pole, and having reached adulthood, complete with the same gray hair and beard as the older elves, Scooter had a heart that still resonated youthful enthusiasm, especially during each Christmas season.

The always-businesslike Piotr, forever sporting his plaid bow-tie over his red fur-coat, stepped forward. "I've already asked the house staff to prepare for the incoming storm. So once they've landed, we should immediately head back to safety."

Knowing nods responded to the Chief of Staff's words.

"There they are!"

Scooter lifted his head back up, his eyes and ears focused as sharp as a hawk's. There it was—a faint rhythm of familiar jingling bells and a tiny but steady red light.

"They're back!"

The crowd burst into busy activity. Hands went into the air, fingers pointing skyward. The animals began hopping about, and the off-duty reindeer stepped forward in anticipation. It wasn't a long wait. The jingle grew louder and the light grew larger and brighter. Soon, the silhouette of the team could be seen through the red-lit clouds and Scooter could feel his pulse quicken with anticipation. Each year, it was the same routine, but the excitement of Santa's return always felt as fresh as the first time.

"Here they come!"

The team flew over the runway, the large red sleigh trailing behind. Almost immediately, Scooter could catch markings of a rough trip—dents and scratches, even a few puncture holes. They touched down and, heading up the slope of the clearing, came to a sliding stop. Aurora and Imo, the two reindeer immediately behind Rudolph, collapsed to the ground while the others drooped their heads and knelt or squatted. Santa himself lay back in his seat and took a deep breath, exhausted.

The crowd of elves and Mrs. Claus rushed over to attend to them. The forest animals crowded around. Old stalwarts Donner and Blitzen ran in to look over the condition of the exhausted reindeer.

"Santa!" several of the elves cried. "Are you all right?"

Scooter stared at the sight in shock. Santa slumped in his chair, a dazed expression on his face.

The reindeer looked as if they had returned from a war and the classic, red sleigh—the apple of Scooter's eye—looked like a battered wreck.

Mrs. Claus clambered into the creaking sleigh, next to Santa and, taking a thick blanket from one of the elves, wrapped and cradled him. "Are you hurt? What happened?"

Santa gazed at her and shook his head. "We're fine, dear. A little tired, but we made it back ahead of the storm."

"We must check you over...."

"Oh no, little woman!"

Seeing Santa push himself up in his seat, Scooter's spirits lifted a little.

"I'm fine," Santa insisted. "Good as gold." Another deep sigh and he collapsed back in his seat.

Scooter had never seen Santa like this before and he couldn't help but note a resemblance between Santa's exhaustion and his reindeers'.

"No, I want Dr. Olaf to be sure of that." Mrs. Claus took Santa's hand and patted it.

"Bah!"

"Now dear, don't be a Scrooge."

"Excuse me." It was Piotr. "We must hurry back before the storm hits."

"Yes," Mrs. Claus agreed. "We must."

Hearing this, Scooter immediately ran forward to help unhitch the poor reindeer. Aurora and Imo remained sprawled on the ground, still too worn out to stand. Scooter paused at the sight of the two helpless deer, touched by how they had obviously given the ride everything they had. While he carefully coaxed the two of them to their feet, Serge loaded the rest of the team onto the carrier sled.

"That's right." Scooter supported Aurora's body while she steadied her legs. After Imo also rose to his feet, Scooter put his arms around their necks and led them forward. "One foot in front of the other. Almost there."

Once they were aboard the carrier and lying down and resting, Scooter signaled the driver to head back to the barn. Serge then restarted the snowmobile and headed away with Piotr while the mighty Donner and Blitzen pulled the sleigh with Santa and Mrs. Claus still together inside back to the castle. The crowd dispersed and as he refastened his cross-country skis for the short walk back, Scooter paused to ponder the moment, deeply disturbed by what had just transpired.

Everyone knew that the modern world could be a dangerous one. But Scooter had never seen it hit this close to home. Not even Santa Claus had been spared.

The howling winds and heavy pounding of hail and sleet echoed throughout the halls of the animal house. The assortment of reindeer lay in their beds of hay and straw, listening to the storm rage outside. Bald-headed Haggen, who was truly as old as a frozen fossil but wasn't really as grumpy as his reputation implied, opened the valve to the geothermal plant to warm the hall, the aroma of organic animal bedding filling the large space. After that, he took a stack of extra blankets and distributed them to the now-resting team. Even with Dancer and Prancer assisting, his creaking joints slowed him to an annoying hobble.

He knelt to check on Aurora and Imo, lying in their straw and recovering from the pounding taken during the ride. "Rest up, little girls." He stroked their necks while he talked to them in his gruff, gritty voice. "You made us all proud." He held Aurora's head while she sipped from her water dish.

Dasher and her young fawn, Holly, walked over to join them.

"Some day," Haggen said to little Holly, "you might be asked to pull Santa's sleigh, too."

Holly cowered back a step.

"Now, don't be afraid," Haggen said. "It's not always this bad. See Aurora and Imo? They're better already. After a good night's sleep, they'll be back to normal. Remember, tomorrow is a new day."

Rudolph wandered over. He was still in good shape and he gently rubbed his now-dimmed nose against the two downed reindeers' faces.

Blankets distributed, Haggen left them to sleep in peace. He headed to the little walkway that joined the animal house to the workshop and joined his rotund sister, Helga.

"Will they be all right?" she asked.

"They'll be fine." His brusque reply didn't sound as confident as it could have.

Helga wrung her hands. "Do you think we made a mistake sending out such a young team?"

Haggen gazed out the small walkway window and stared at the harrowing flurries blowing about, outside.

"Maybe we should have brought back a couple of the older ones," she continued. "If not Donner and Blitzen, then perhaps Dancer and Prancer."

Haggen glanced back at the sleeping reindeer, remembering the year of the Great Blizzard—the year Santa first pressed a young but powerful Rudolph and his beacon-like noselight into service. That storm was so hazardous and extensive that Haggen had to pull the rest of the younger reindeer off duty in favor of the original "A" team.

"Maybe you're right." He nodded sadly before pulling on his stocking cap to head home. "Our young ones would have been greatly disappointed, but it would not have been as risky as it turned out."

Scooter watched the team of chatty materials engineers leave the hall, his face struggling to hold back tears. The hour was very late and he pulled at his suspenders in frustration. He loved the old sleigh. It was a classic from uncounted years past, cleaned and polished with immaculate care, and restored to its original pristine condition every year. He personally revarnished the surface, inch by inch.

They didn't make them like this anymore, with real wood and metal frames. The modern world used plastic and an occasional metal-alloy, probably laced with an assortment of carcinogenic by-products. He tried to compose himself. "Young" as he was, he was a senior mechanic and he had a job to do. Scooter glanced at his report and sank into a mire of dark desperation.

Wide-bodied Bjork waddled into the shop, his thick-lensed, taped-up glasses sliding low on his nose, his clipboard swinging in his arm.

"Good evening, Scooter," the head of engineering said with a matter-of-fact air. "Do you have your assessment?"

"Yes. It's not good." Scooter spoke in a flat, dispassionate monotone. "The sleigh took a tremendous beating. It looks like it went through a violent hailstorm, perhaps more than one. There are pockmarks all over and punch holes throughout the frame. The skids are bent. There may have been several rough landings. One side is very badly dented, as if it sideswiped a chimney, or satellite dish, or both."

Bjork grunted as he took notes on his clipboard. "Repair estimate?"

Scooter tried to keep his focus. "I can't say for sure. Weeks. Perhaps...m-m-m...."

Bjork nodded and took off his glasses. "Can I see?"

Scooter sighed. "Follow me." He led Bjork into

the repair bay where the sleigh sat, exactly as he had described it. They both gazed at the wreckage in silence. Finally, unable to hold it in any longer, Scooter broke down.

"My poor bairns!" he cried.

Santa's recovery was slow. Dr. Olaf attributed this to natural aging, something that did not sit well with Santa.

"Now, don't be a stubborn old goat," Mrs. Claus reminded him after Olaf left.

"Goats are strong and agile," Santa retorted. "Mules are stubborn."

He rested up, then began taking short walks to regain his strength. After a few weeks, he felt strong enough to bring out his cross-country skis and embark on longer trips through the surrounding regions.

Everyone took a vacation in the spring. With Christmas over, and the rest of the world stressed about making their credit card payments, no one thought about requesting next year's presents, yet. In the old days, the elves continued their work to build up the inventory. But with new efficiencies and following modern best practices, they now devoted the first part of the year to committee work, brainstorming innovations and improvements.

Santa, meanwhile, took day trips throughout the northern lands, sometimes with Mrs. Claus, sometimes alone. Sometimes, he would take parties of elves with him; other times, he would take teams of reindeer on training runs.

One day, he neared the northernmost farmlands, alone. It was an area he frequented when he first arrived in the North from Asia Minor, many, many years ago. Things hadn't changed much, despite all of the modernizations that had occurred in the industrialized parts of the North. It was still a simple agrarian life, with animals, not machines, doing the heavy work.

In the fields, workers in heavy, all-weather coats prepared the fields for spring planting, breaking the ice and snow and tilling the soil. One by one, they looked up and waved or shouted a greeting toward Santa. With a smile and a sense of accomplishment, Santa skied to a stop and plunged his poles into the ground. Soon, a small and haggard-looking old man limped out of his house. With a pointy-toothed smile beaming from his crusty face, he embraced Santa.

"St. Nicholas!" His smoky voice boomed, the horns on his head long shriveled away. "What brings you back to our humble home? It's been a long time."

"Farmer Ruprecht." Santa gave a wide smile, jolly as only he could be. "I've come to exercise my legs and visit an old friend."

"Your old humble servant," Ruprecht corrected.

"And my old friend," Santa corrected.

"Come inside—we have a lot to catch up."

Together, they went straight to the kitchen, and the liquor cabinet. Ruprecht bypassed the ales and pulled out two bottles of brandy. "Monk liquors, always the best for Santa. Red or green?"

"Green for growth," Santa pointed.

"Yes." Ruprecht laughed. "Santa likes the stronger proof." He poured two glasses and passed one to Santa. "To your health." He raised his glass.

"Thank you." Santa also lifted his glass. "And to your health, as well."

They clanked and drank heartily.

Santa paused, his eyes bulging, the full blast and burn of the liquor almost knocking him over. That was good.

"So, why do you still do it?" Ruprecht asked, not mincing any words. "We pick up the satellite news up here, like you do. Every year, the children become less and less deserving and more able to simply buy what they want, whether they're behaving or not. What do they ask you for, these days? Computers? Combat games? Smart phones? Those aren't toys, not the simple pleasures of childhood. And they aren't rewards for being good little boys and girls, either."

Santa was amused at his old, outspoken friend. Amused and reflective of his words. "Sometimes I wonder, myself. Maybe the time has come for me to think about retirement."

Ruprecht took a long drink. "Retiring isn't going to solve anything. Somebody needs to set the kids straight."

"What would you suggest?"

"For one thing, bring back the birch sticks."

Santa shook his head. "No." Absolutely not.

"The coal, then. Bring back the coal."

Santa could see that Ruprecht was dead serious.

"At the very least, introduce a modern day equivalent, like a recycled disc. Something so they know that they didn't deserve anything from Santa, this year. Or, let me come with you again, like before. If you haven't the heart to scold the rotten apples, then let me play the bad cop."

Santa shook his head a second time. "You know I can't do that anymore." He quickly added, "And you can't be hauling children off in that old bag of yours either."

"You've gotten soft in your old age."

"Ruprecht, my friend..." Santa put his hand on Ruprecht's shoulder. "...my old friend, my dear old friend, what if I made a mistake and gave a lump of coal to the wrong child? I don't think I could live with that on my conscience. Do you understand?" Now Santa was serious. "It's a complicated world out there."

Ruprecht smirked. "Too complicated, if you ask me. I like it here, where it's simple." He eyed Santa. "Take a word of advice from me. One of these days, your sleigh is going to get fleeced while you're inside laying presents. For Pete's sake, get an alarm, will you?"

2. *The Cruiser*

Scooter set his bags down and gazed out the oversized windows of the old elf lodge, admiring the serenity of Lake Puck. It was time for the annual three-day elf convocation, when the entire community retreated back to their old home village and took up residence under the ancient timbers of the old lodge. There, they swam and fished and discussed the major initiatives for the upcoming year. Usually, new toy innovations dominated the agenda. This year, though, Bjork and his staff from the garage had a major proposal which Bjork would present at the first combined session. Scooter took off his plaid coat and hustled for his room. He had a lot of setup to do.

At the combined session, Bjork stood before the elf audience that sat around the expansive stone amphitheater in the center of the lodge while Scooter manned the projector booth.

"As we all know," Bjork addressed the elves, "we are in the 21st century, and the outside world has changed with the times. The last few years, these changes have made Santa's annual Christmas Eve ride more and more perilous. The skies are now filled with planes, satellites, and other air traffic. Global warming has increased both the frequency and intensity of major winter weather systems and storms. And every year, Santa and the reindeer team have returned more tossed and battered than ever."

Scooter nodded in agreement. He had inspected how devastating the damage had been. Now, the rest of the community would find out, too.

Bjork waved his hand at the booth and Scooter dimmed the lights and brought up the first projector image. A picture of Santa's battered hulk, sitting in the garage, appeared on the front screen, drawing a loud chorus of gasps.

"Meanwhile, the population is still growing," Bjork continued. "The number of children, and therefore, the length and complexity of Santa's trip, continues to increase dramatically. This year, the cost of repairing the sleigh has become prohibitive. For these reasons, and simply to aid Santa in improving both the efficiency and comfort of his world travels, we propose retiring the old sleigh and designing and building a new state-of-the-art model, to be used this coming Christmas Eve."

Scooter advanced the slide and held his breath. Here it comes. The screen switched to a computer drawing of a sleek, rocket-like vehicle, with a likeness of Santa in the capsule. "Ooo's" and "ahh's" could be heard as the elves took in the picture and its implications.

Bjork held out his hand. "Presenting, Santa's cruiser."

Slowly, a round of applause began to build and spread until it rippled throughout the entire lodge. Scooter shut off the projector and brought up the lights. There were many nodding heads in the crowd and several side conversations.

One old elf in dark blue coveralls stood off to the side with his arms folded, silent and unsmiling. Haggen. Scooter knew this wasn't a good sign. Haggen was old as dirt and eternally grumpy, but the hard stare in his eyes felt different. Haggen didn't like the rocket.

After the meeting, Scooter hurriedly packed up the presentation materials, then set out in search of Haggen. He always had a soft spot for the crotchety old chief herdsman. Haggen always offered the elf children the chance to handle the young deer, something few took, given Haggen's reputation and the multitude of surplus toys at the toy factory competing for attention. Those who did—such as a curious Scooter—got to see a very different Haggen, though, one who cared and nurtured the animals with a gentle hand, a tender voice, and a kind heart. Over the years, Haggen grew even more cantankerous, but Scooter never forgot the other man inside.

He found Haggen at the Ice House, sitting alone at the counter, staring at his half-full glass, brooding. Strange murmurs rumbled out his mouth —musings of departing with the entire herd for real Nature, where they could eat and be eaten. Very strange, indeed.

Scooter approached Haggen. "Mind if I join you?"

Haggen stared at him but did not utter a sound.

Not hearing anything that suggested a "no" answer, Scooter pulled out the seat next to Haggen, sat down, and ordered an ale. There, they stayed silent for a long time.

Scooter's mind drifted to thoughts about the old sleigh and his feelings for it. When he was a boy, Scooter had told everyone within shouting distance that he wanted to be an engineer, not a toymaker. He spent his free time studying the history of snow sleighs, especially Santa's centuries-old modified Albany cutter, and he fostered ambitions of founding his own engineering firm and building Santa a clean, modern replica.

But for now, he was just a senior mechanic, and there was the rocket announcement, a different replacement than what he had dreamed of, and Scooter became aware of his ambivalence toward the proposal.

He glanced at Haggen and a light bulb went off about the old herdsman. Finally, Scooter uttered, "I know how you feel. I feel the same way."

Haggen looked at him. "How would you know how I feel?" Cold spit landed on Scooter's face.

Scooter could tell that Haggen had very strong feelings about the cruiser rocket—stronger than his own. On the one hand, Haggen's reindeer would no longer be exposed to the dangerous elements or the increasingly crowded air traffic. But on the other hand—or maybe it was actually the same hand, Scooter thought to himself as he peeked out the window at the herd feeding in the snow-covered meadow—they would no longer be needed at all. Like the old classic sleigh, the reindeer would no longer have a part in bringing Santa's gifts to the children of the world.

"I can't wait to go home with the reindeer," Haggen muttered. "It can't end soon enough. It's one thing for the toy-makers to adopt new technologies." He swallowed a swag. "But replacing the entire team of reindeer is an outrage."

Scooter realized that Haggen's feelings had turned into resentment.

Haggen was brought back to the here and now by a nudge from behind. Scooter recognized young Holly, who had wandered in, hoping for a treat.

"Sorry, girl," Haggen said to her. "I didn't think to bring anything special for you, today. My mind was still on that blasted rocket." His hand gently cupped her chin. "I'll be sure to bring you some, tomorrow. Okay, girl?"

He gave her head a tender pat and sent her back outside. "Dasher's feeding in the meadow," Haggen muttered to Scooter. "Her father, Comet, is out there, too." He blew out his breath. "So, half of the herd of fifty are grazing and half are sleeping in the animal house."

Haggen looked Scooter in the eye. "Tell me, boy —is this the life the reindeer have to look forward to? Eating, sleeping, occasionally reproducing...?"

An emptiness filled Scooter's heart and his mind turned back to the old sleigh, which would not even be able to eat or reproduce, only sleep.

Santa and Mrs. Claus woke up bright and early and immediately walked out onto their balcony in their baby-blue flannel robes to greet the morning sun that rose over the polar icecaps. It was the first day of summer, the day targeted for the big experiment. Many from the elf community were already out on the frozen meadow. Haggen and the herd gathered at one end of the field. Serge and his staff worked in their make-shift command center on the far end of a marked-off "runway," making final preparations while Bjork hovered over them, pacing. Meanwhile, the toymakers crowded the roof of their low-slung shop, overlooking the valley meadow.

"Would you like an early breakfast, sir?" asked Piotr, the Chief of Staff. "Everybody is already up. It's a big day and nobody wanted to miss it."

"Let's wait until the launch is over," Santa said, sitting down. He didn't feel hungry, this morning.

"Very good, sir." Piotr excused himself and left just as Dr. Olaf arrived.

"Good morning, Dr. Olaf," Mrs. Claus greeted. "Here to watch the launch with us?"

"And to check how Santa is doing, this morning." Olaf put his black bag down on the breakfast table and breathed in the crisp, morning air.

Santa stifled a grumble. "Slept like a baby."

"And how are you feeling?" Olaf asked. "Excited? Ambivalent? Hostile?"

Santa sighed. "I'm keeping an open mind." It was truthful, if not complete. Santa had a bad feeling about this.

Bjork's voice came over the PA system. "Please clear the launch site. T-minus three minutes and counting."

Santa stared at the rocket. "My, my...." It was very tall. Three large boosters, protruding from the bottom, warmed up while five retro-burners lined their perimeter. A series of flaps and fins extended about halfway up the side. Behind them was a ring of four-way steering rockets. A transparent capsule sat at the top with a mannequin of Santa inside and the red beacon at the tip. Someone had stenciled the name of the rocket in bold red paint on one side: *North Star*.

"T-minus one minute."

"It's quite an accomplishment," Olaf remarked with a smile.

"But will it work?" Santa asked. "It's a big step, going from toy rockets to the real thing."

"You just said you would keep an open mind," Mrs. Claus reminded him. "Don't you want this to succeed?"

"Of course!" Santa paused. "But it's very risky and I don't want to think about the ramifications of failing." Fleeting thoughts filled his mind. "Did it pass all of the simulation tests? Shouldn't they postpone this until it's rock solid, to be sure?"

"Don't be silly!" Mrs. Claus scolded.

"This would certainly help with your physical longevity," Olaf said. "No more battering rides on the old sleigh."

Santa sighed. "How many G-forces does it do? Can you see me wearing a helmet?"

Mrs. Claus stared at him. "Actually, I think I could."

"Thirty seconds."

Santa defiantly put his feet up on the tabletop surface and looked around at the crowd of elf engineers running about their little command post. All except for one, he noticed. Scooter stood a short distance to one side, watching.

"Fifteen seconds."

"Clear out!" Serge's voice cut in over the speakers.

As the time ticked down, everybody scrambled

to the perimeter of the meadow, the engineers evacuating the command post and Haggen leading the herd to the edge of the woods, leaving the test rocket to stand alone in the launch area. Everybody except Scooter, who remained as he had been, watching up close.

"Five,...four,...three,...two,...one...."

The boosters roared to life with a gigantic plume of black smoke, lifting the rocket slowly upward, off the ground. Cheers erupted from the elves as Serge announced over his microphone, "We have lift-off!" For a moment, even Santa had a sense of awe of what he was witnessing. This was real progress, real achievement.

Then, the steering rockets fired to take the vessel away, into the sky. Or rather, they misfired— the *North Star* veered off at a wild angle, its steering rockets sputtering intermittently. Screams erupted from the crowd. Without warning, one of the rockets suddenly ignited and it swung around in a wide arc, skimming the treetops and heading straight for the elves. They ducked out of the way as it swooped past them, then back up and away toward the workshop building. The toy-makers quickly evacuated the roof as it roared past them and flew toward the castle.

"Look out!" Santa heard Olaf cry out.

Serge ran headlong over a cowering Bjork, back to the command post, and hit an emergency destruct switch. Explosive bolts fired, breaking all of the components of the rocket apart. The engines exploded and debris showered down on the castle grounds, including the still-intact Santa mannequin, which landed on the castle roof with a hard bounce.

Like that, it was over. The stench of black rocket smoke drifted in the air as the concussion from the explosions echoed throughout the valley. The cries of the panicked animals trailed away into the distance.

Olaf peeked out from the balcony's French door. Mrs. Claus lifted her head from behind her oversized patio chair. Santa only grunted with mixed emotions. He knew it wouldn't work, but it was still painful to see all of the hard work fail.

"Well," he said, changing the subject, "maybe I'll have breakfast."

Chaos engulfed the meeting room and Bjork struggled to restore order. Everybody talked all at once, some with raised voices, hypothesizing what could have gone wrong. Even Serge argued heatedly with the head of the toy division. The only person not caught in the vocal sparring was Scooter, who watched in deep contemplation.

The year was half over and they had no sleigh for Santa, new or old. Further, with all of the reassignments for the construction of the prototype rocket, they were now behind schedule on toy production. Scooter considered undertaking a personal initiative to restore the old sleigh back to working condition. Again. It wouldn't afford Santa any more protection than last Christmas Eve, but at least he would be flying. Unsure of what to do, he glanced at Serge, who was now surrounded by three minions from the toy division.

The door opened and Santa walked in. Upon seeing his presence, Bjork raised his arms and managed to hush the crowd.

Santa looked to Bjork, then said to everybody in his deep, rich voice, "Please be seated."

Slowly, the elves settled down, many seated, but many also left standing around the perimeter, including Scooter.

"Thank you," Santa began. He gave everyone a heartfelt smile, then pulled over a stool and sat down. "I know how hard everybody worked on the *North Star*, and how deeply disappointed everybody must be, after this morning's accident, and I wanted everyone to know how grateful both Mrs. Claus and I are for your efforts to ensure my safety."

There was something in listening to Santa's voice that soothed Scooter. He instinctively sat down on the floor and made himself comfortable, as he did when he was a young boy.

"If you do choose to continue with this project, I would request that it not be too great of a departure from what I am already using." Santa sighed. "You are working with an old man who is comfortable doing what he has always done. My ability to pick up the new technologies is very limited. So please, no more self-propelled high-altitude rockets. I would be more than happy to have a traditional reindeer-pulled sleigh with upgraded protection. That would be plenty of improvement for me."

He rose from his stool and held out his hands. "So do not be discouraged, and do not feel that you have wasted a half year's work. I will have something special for each of you for this effort, at the end of the year. Thank you, from the bottom of my heart."

Scooter did not feel discouraged at all. His thoughts turned to Haggen and the herd, who were now back in the picture. Haggen should be happy with this news. Then, as he watched Santa exit the meeting room, he realized that he had no clue what did this mean for his own work. Old sleigh or new —or both? They didn't have much time to figure it out.

3. Flight Tests

News spread like wildfire through the community. By far, the most excited were Haggen and the reindeer herders. He gimped out into the field, the herd of fifty-some reindeer charging at full sprint alongside, whooping and hollering with excitement. With a few brief words from Santa, their sense of purpose was renewed, and the annual training games—the two-week athletic competition of strength and speed, comprised of a staggering array of running, jumping, and pulling events, and embellished with parades and pageantry—took on an energy not seen since their inauguration.

At the garage, though, it was back to the drawing board for Serge, Scooter, and the other mechanics. Sadly, the old sleigh still sat to one side, unrepaired, now serving as a model for a new sleigh. But to Scooter's satisfaction, Serge settled on retaining the same basic shape for the new and improved model.

Among the staff, Beavo built panels to house electronic brains and other circuitry while Jimbub added creature comforts such as hot and cold snack compartments. Serge focused on installing a convertible top to protect Santa from the violent elements of the sky. No longer would Santa be at the mercy of the snowstorms, the freezing rain, and the arctic wind gusts. In addition, a large, oversized chair, clothed in rich Corinthian leather and sporting full tilt and swivel controls, lumbar support, and dual cupholders, was ordered from an elf village in Northern Sweden. Even the electronic toy division contributed a simple computerized database, for use as Santa's list of good and bad children.

Scooter, meanwhile, was tasked with designing and adding an instrument dashboard, steering gear that controlled the reins, and a parking brake that released and retracted a spiked anchor. How he ended up with such a broad, all-encompassing job, he wasn't sure. But he was glad to be working on the closest thing to his childhood dream. This would be a cool, modern sleigh.

If he could figure out how to pull it off, that was.

Scooter rolled up his sleeves and enthusiastically plunged in like a true engineer, appropriating a used CAD station and downloading designs from around the world. As the weeks passed, he could see the new sleigh begin to take shape. The anchor was simple and quick, a straight-forward mechanical addition. The steering gear was more complex. Because he didn't know how many reindeer would be used, he had to make it an expandable control. But by far, the most difficult component was the dashboard. The possibilities were intriguing, and he spent countless hours daydreaming the number of gauges to include and what they would be monitoring—location and altitude, weather, whatever else—but as he realized that he was stuck on finding a suitable onboard power source, his enthusiasm waned from the weight of reality.

Late summer brought the day of the new test flight. Serge and his boys scurried about, checking out all of the major sections of the still-unpainted sleigh while Scooter hurriedly tightened all of the bolts, one by one. The dashboard was still not ready, but fortunately, it wouldn't be needed for today. Only a single gauge—the altimeter—functioned, and that only because Scooter had loaded a very heavy battery pack in the rear of the sleigh.

Just then, he saw Haggen bring four reindeer out of the animal house to hitch up and a thought entered Scooter's mind. "Oh-oh." He ran over to Bjork and asked, "Do we know how much heavier this new sleigh is? We packed a lot into it."

Bjork peered at him over his glasses and lowered his clipboard, his brow furled. "No one brought this up before. We all thought the new, lightweight alloys would actually make the sleigh lighter, not heavier." He turned away and called over to Serge, who was adjusting the Captain's chair. "How is it up there?"

Serge, playing with the controls, gave a thumbs up and a smile.

Scooter swallowed, hoping for the best as he watched Haggen hook up the four young reindeer, Storm, Hayley, Thor, and Sirius. Serge tightened the steering gear, retracted the anchor, and directed the reindeer to turn the sleigh around so that it was pointed down the runway markers.

"Ready!" he called out.

Bjork, backed by the engineering staff, returned Serge's thumbs up.

Serge eased the shifter forward and the sleigh started down the runway, the four reindeer gathering speed as momentum built. While an assistant pointed the radar gun, Scooter kept his eye on the remote speed monitor, anticipating when the sleigh would reach take-off velocity. Halfway down the runway, the team was still accelerating. But as they approached the end marker, Serge had to throttle back and bring the team to a stop.

"Slush!" Scooter muttered. They were going to need more reindeer.

Soon, Haggen added two more-muscular bucks, Speed and Slick, and the exercise was repeated, going the other way, with the same result. He brought out two even-more-powerful pullers, Pounder and St. Lucius. Finally, with Night-Train and Tank added to make the team total ten reindeer, they were able to achieve take-off velocity. Two by two, the mighty reindeer leaped skyward with the sleigh still on the ground, dragging behind them.

Scooter started to giggle at the sight but muffled it with the realization that this was going nowhere, and his dead-weight battery pack wasn't helping.

Bjork brought in old, shriveled Professor Skye, who pulled his custom-made slide-rule out of his coat pocket and began recalculating the take-off speed. While they worked, Scooter ran over to the sleigh and consulted with Serge.

"What are we going to do when Santa climbs in and we've also added the toys to the hold?" Scooter asked.

"[expletive deleted]" Serge blew out his breath. "We'll have to have a longer runway and even more muscular reindeer. Tell Haggen to change some of the team out for some bigger boys."

"I'll see what we can do," Scooter replied, turning away to get Haggen.

Haggen grumbled at Scooter's request. "Bah! This is progress, boy?" He shook his head and proceeded to unfasten the hitches. "I'm sorry, kids." Stroking their necks, Haggen replaced Storm, Hayley, Sirius, Speed, Slick, and St. Lucius with experienced veterans Dancer and Prancer and powerful pullers Donner, Blitzen, and Rudolph.

Scooter watched Haggen lead the young reindeer away, and he felt disappointed for them.

Meanwhile, additional markers were set out in the big meadow to form a new and longer, though not as flat, runway. By the time everything was ready for the launch attempt, the sun had already set behind the distant mountains.

Scooter nervously crossed his fingers as Haggen returned to watch. This had been a long day and nobody knew when it would end.

"Lights!" Serge called to Rudolph, who brightened up his nose for the now-nighttime launch. He pushed the shifter forward and the team started down the makeshift runway. As they charged downhill, they quickly achieved take-off velocity. Then the bowl-shaped meadow changed to an upward slope. When they reached the apex, Rudolph and the girls launched themselves into the air, followed by the four young ones. The mighty Donner and Blitzen then gave the overweight sleigh one final, hard pull and together, they all went airborne.

"Yeah!" cried Scooter as Serge waved down at the cheering crowd.

Once the sleigh achieved altitude, it flew almost as gracefully as the old sleigh did. Serge directed the team to make two wide circles over the meadow. Then as they headed off for a flyby of the castle, Scooter offered Haggen a high-five.

* * *

"The weather station is picking up a large storm system ahead," Scooter reported.

"Understood." Santa's head swung from one side of the console to the other.

"Recommend you swing around the system, rather than fly through it."

"Understood."

"Switch to tactical course control," the computer voice directed over the speaker. "New heading coming up."

Suddenly, the flashing collision alarm began blaring, just as the new heading registered on the dashboard.

"Incoming—hard to starboard...!" Scooter tensed.

"What?" Santa pulled back on the steering gear.

"Right!" Scooter yelled. "Turn right!"

"Whoa!" Santa exclaimed, as a bright red light enveloped him. "...what happened?"

There was a long pause. Scooter didn't know how to break the news to Santa. "You got hit by a jumbo jet that was emerging from the storm cloud, sir."

Santa blinked as the red light faded, leaving him in darkness. "Am I dead?"

"Yes, sir. I'm sorry, sir."

Santa grumbled. "Not half as sorry as I."

The door opened and Bjork and Serge joined Scooter in the control booth. While he slowly took off his headset and dialed up the lights, the two bosses stared at each other with blank expressions.

"Shall we try again?" Bjork ventured.

"Again?" Serge asked. "This will be his ninth attempt."

Bjork shook his head in resignation. "There has to be another way."

Scooter looked through the window at a noticeably frustrated Santa, whose head sank to a rest on his hands. For an instant, Scooter flashed back to a childhood memory—he didn't even remember how old he was—of Santa handing him a Christmas present. It was a model sleigh, an exact replica of Santa's, and the instant he touched it and held it in his hands, Scooter experienced visions of someday handling the real thing. But Scooter also remembered how young-at-heart Santa had been, how his eyes sparkled and his rosy cheeks shone in the lamplight. There was an unmistakable aura radiating about Santa, a liveliness that felt timeless. Young Scooter knew that Santa was elderly, but not old.

But now, the Santa who sat in the simulator room did look old, very old and worn out. Now, Scooter finally understood what Santa had meant during his brief speech at the convocation. He wished he could wave a magic wand and restore Santa back to his prime, or take the weight of the modern world off of Santa's shoulders. But the modern world was a realist world, a world without magic.

"Scooter?" Serge interrupted. "Any more ideas...?"

"More reindeer?" Helga exclaimed as she bathed little Mo in the far corner of the animal house. "They need even more reindeer, now? What are they thinking?"

Haggen stood over them with two buckets of warm water in his hands. He nodded his head, silently brooding at the new decision coming out of engineering. Haggen set down the buckets and gave her the fur towels he carried on his shoulder.

"They're making the sleigh even bigger," he said in a crabby tone, "so that one of the elves can ride with Santa and operate all of the fancy new equipment."

"What?" Helga asked. "A chauffeur?"

Haggen snorted and turned away. As he strolled among the many young reindeer in the animal house, he noticed young Holly, playing with a butterfly that had somehow wandered in from the field. He didn't want to keep reusing the old pros, but he didn't see how this was going to work with inexperienced flyers. He put his snowcap on, reached out, and tapped Bounder and Brawny on their shoulders. "Come, ol' boys, we need your help."

Soon, he had a dozen reindeer lined up at the start of the runway in six pairs. Behind them sat the modified, two-wide sleigh with Serge inside, monitoring the complex instruments. Bjork and Scooter stood at the observation point, awaiting the takeoff.

"Let's go!" Haggen called out, encouraging the team. He climbed into the driver's seat, playing Santa, next to Serge. This was the first try of the day and everyone wondered if things would progress any better than the all-day exercise, two weeks ago. Well, Haggen determined, if anyone was going to lead the reindeer to triumph, it would be him. Him or no one.

The runway had been extended even further with the use of a wooden extension ramp. The end of the ramp was elevated to maintain the same angle of elevation over the descending ground. The effect was the same as jumping off a ski-jump or an aircraft carrier. Or a cliff.

"Charge!" Haggen roared to the team. They barreled ahead and leaped over the drop-off, into the sky. "Yeah!" He raised his fist in triumph as they climbed into the daylight in a wide, graceful arc.

They made several circles over the field, then headed for a flyby over the castle, where Haggen waved to Santa and Mrs. Claus as they ate breakfast on the balcony with Dr. Olaf.

One problem solved—and a new one for Scooter to tackle. Not many rooftops were the length of a runway, but the old sleigh was able to land practically on a dime and be pulled almost vertically straight up into the sky by the reindeer team. The new sleigh, on the other hand, was so heavy that that kind of precision wasn't possible, anymore. He couldn't help but start to feel resentment that the old sleigh had been abandoned as unceremoniously as it had.

Scooter stood up from his computer station and walked to the basin to splash cold water on his face. The battery pack had to go, obviously, but the only portable power source that could last a round-the-world journey was the breeder reactor, where they grew deuterium for the physical plant. He'd have to fabricate a lead container—even heavier than the battery pack—for a pellet.

Splash! The cold water was jarring. Scooter took a deep breath. Focus on the new sleigh, not the old.

So, how could he make the sleigh do a vertical take-off without reverting back to the rocket? He found himself wishing for a magic wand that could transport Santa to the rooftop without having to land the sleigh at all. Scooter sighed and splashed his face a second time. Childhood fantasies. He wiped his face dry and returned to his workstation, grim with determination.

Finally, after poring over research documents, historical articles, and news footage for two solid weeks, he re-emerged, bleary-eyed but rejuvenated with excitement, with a proposal for Serge and Bjork borrowed from the old days of NASA.

"Very interesting," Bjork said after reading Scooter's notes. "What do you think, Serge?"

Serge's eyes darted from top to bottom of his copy of Scooter's notes. "I think this could work, as long as the power apparatus holds up." He put the notes down and looked at Bjork. "Honestly, sir, we're running out of time and this would appear to be our only workable solution."

Bjork grunted. "It would seem so." He glanced at Scooter, who anxiously waited for the final decision. "Approved for development." With that, he turned and left.

Serge put his hand on Scooter's shoulder and said, "Good job. You may have just saved Christmas. I'll go call a staff meeting."

Scooter watched Serge disappear into the hallway, exhausted but internally elated that he, and he alone, had found a way to make Santa's new sleigh work.

"Ready for docking maneuver," Haggen radioed. This would be an interesting experience, he thought to himself.

He flew the sleigh in a wide, circular holding pattern over the meadow. In the rear, Serge approached in a small, one-man sleigh pulled by Donner. Haggen looked down to the ground and saw Scooter, Bjork, and the staff huddled around the large field command center.

"All right," Serge said over the speaker. "Here

we come."

"Not too fast," Bjork cut in. "Keep tight control."

"Understood," Serge answered.

"One hundred meters to go," Scooter reported.

"I see him," Haggen said into his microphone. "He's right below me." He saw several of the reindeer raise their heads in excitement. "Steady, boys, just hold it steady and let Donner do all the work." He got several head nods in reply. Reindeer are always so understanding.

"Fifty meters."

"Latches open," Haggen said as he flipped a row of switches on the dashboard.

"All right, Donner," Serge said over the radio. "Nice and smooth, now. That's the way to do it. Nice and smooth."

"Ten meters...five..."

Haggen held his breath in anticipation. He was counting on good old dependable Donner to bring Serge in without crashing. They were now flying parallel, close enough for Haggen to reach out and touch the other sleigh.

"Three, two, one...."

There was a slight thud as they made contact, and then Haggen flipped the control to lock the three latches with loud metallic snaps. Over the speaker, cheers erupted. Haggen felt a wave of relief. They were now flying as one combined sleigh—the mothership and a lander.

"Great job, guys," Bjork said.

Great job by the reindeer, Haggen thought to himself, proud of his team.

The last of the elves headed out, some for home, others to the Blue Ice tavern for a drink. The electronic toy division had installed the final element, the toy and gift library computer, in the morning and thoroughly tested and debugged all afternoon and into the evening. Now, the last members of the wash-and-shine crew gathered their equipment and headed back to their shop, finished for the night.

Santa entered the empty garage with soft footsteps. He was dressed in an old flannel shirt, suspenders, and a loose jacket with a gray stocking hat over his bald head, and his reading glasses still hung low over his nose. The only trace of seasonal clothing was his favorite belt—something he always wore loosely for sentiment, since his suspenders actually held his pants up. The buckle was a metal casting of the Greek letters alpha and omega, a gift from a silversmith when he was still a bishop in Turkey, and he always wore it as a reminder of his innermost, personal faith.

Santa stood in front of what remained of the old sleigh, which not only had not been repaired, but actually had some parts salvaged during the construction of the new sleigh. For example, the runners had been removed, melted down, straightened back out, lined with electric heating coils, and mounted on the new sleigh. The old bench seat was gone, now rebuilt as a new cargo bay for the toy inventory. He took out his pipe, lit it, and stood there, lost in thought, recalling many fond memories and many treasured rides around the world.

Finally, he stepped over to the new sleigh, which sat in silence, polished and dried. He gazed at it, looking over all of the new gadgets and features. It was a three-car design, based on the old motorcycle sidecar. The left sidecar, to be pulled by a single reindeer, had been designated the lander for Santa to shuttle between the circling sleigh and all of the homes he would be visiting. The right sidecar, also pulled by a single reindeer, was for the elf assistant—to be named, shortly—piloting the sleigh while it was in holding pattern. He would handle the advanced electronics and the weather station, and feed the reindeer, using the robotic arm purchased from the same Canadian company that made the robotic arms used on the old space shuttle and the international space station.

Two railings soared around the interior compartment of the sleigh, tracks for the retractable top, to insulate Santa from any bad weather encountered. Finally, all of the advanced features and equipment were powered by a small, sealed core, a pellet-sized version of the lead-shielded deuterium reactor that served as the physical plant for the castle and powered the network grid to the surrounding compounds. For now, the power core was dark, and the sleigh sat in silence.

Santa climbed in and sat down in the big chair, making himself comfortable. He took out two small items from his oversized jacket and mounted them in the two empty slots in the dashboard. One was a porcelain portrait of his wife, made by an old elf, years ago. The other was a plaque given to him when he left Turkey to begin his missionary work among the children. It was a small nativity engraving and the accompanying passage from Luke which quoted the angels' chorus: "Glory to God in the highest; and peace on earth and goodwill toward men."

Haggen downed his fifth ale. If he had something stronger, he would have drunk that, instead. He held out his empty mug. "Another!"

"Haggen!"

He turned his head. It was Helga, bundled up for the long walk back to her home, making her way over from the door of the near-empty Blue Ice tavern.

She glared at him. "What are you doing?"

Haggen paused. His arms had finally stopped shaking.

Helga looked him over. "Nervous about the weather report?" she asked, her voice disarmingly soft as she pulled the mug out of his hand.

"Bah! They didn't bother to put in any creature comforts for the reindeer, did they?" He snorted. It was the end of December again, and the terrifying northern storm fronts had rapidly reformed in the last few days. "Did you notice?"

Helga nodded as she put the mug aside.

"Santa and his elf-pilot will be well-protected from the storms." He looked at her. "But what about our little ones?" Haggen went silent as he eyed Bjork ambling into the Blue Ice. It was the stare of the evil eye.

"Haggen," Helga said, her voice low, "he was only doing his job. Don't blame him for something that's not his fault."

"No," Haggen groused. "He wanted a rocket. Have you forgotten? Engineers, they love to change things. We were the only ones who wanted the deer to keep flying."

He went silent again, sulking as he watched Bjork order a drink and walk out with it. Less than a minute later, Scooter walked in, sat down in the same seat Bjork had vacated, and placed an order of his own.

Haggen turned back to Helga. "Why couldn't they have built an automatic blanket draper or something like that? Or made helmets shaped for a reindeer's head?"

Helga shook her head with a smile. "You're being silly. Reindeer are heartier than Santa. Protecting him was the goal of the new sleigh. Like the Pope's car, right?" She offered a lighthearted laugh.

"The *Popemobile*?"

"You have to admit," Helga continued. "Santa is a little like our Pope."

Haggen was outraged by what he heard and his heart burned with anger. Yes, Santa was like a father to everyone, old and young. He was timeless and magical. But—"Reindeer are no less valuable, Helga!"

"Haggen, lower your voice—"

She shot a quick glance at Scooter, looking their way, seeming to have overheard.

"Was it too much to ask?" Undeterred, Haggen continued his rant with a snarl. "They could have programmed the *Santamobile*'s feed arm to drape and wrap protective blankets around the reindeer. Heck, why not divert power from the core to raise a deflector?"

Helga threw up her hands. "You've been watching too many reruns, Haggen." She lowered her voice, again. "And you've had too many ales to think straight. Go home and get some sleep."

Scooter spoke up, stepping over. "Can I offer you a ride home?"

Haggen paused with a stupefied look on his face. "Huh?" His mind felt like mush. "What am I doing here?" He looked at Helga and Scooter, his face going blank for a second. "Bah! I should be with my reindeer. I'll go stay with them, tonight."

"Haggen, you're not a reindeer," Helga scolded, "you're an elf."

"I just...." Haggen faltered, struggling to gathered his thoughts. "I wish I could be sure that they'll be okay."

Helga sighed. "Then why don't you ask to be the elf driver? You'd done some of the tests, and you said the fancy gadgets weren't all that complicated."

Haggen cocked his head. "You really think so?"

4. *Some Things Never Change*

Santa and Mrs. Claus ate in silence. As he dabbled in his food, Santa pored over the thick stack of demographics reports, an update from last year's edition. Sprawled over the table were the annual intelligence reports from around the world on the activities of the children, broken down by city and county, and by age, and the annual inventory report from the toy shop. Unable to finish his dinner, Santa put his fork down.

His wife seized the moment to ask him, "Is something troubling you? You look distracted."

Santa sighed. "Look at this. Demographics reports, intelligence reports, weather reports." He pointed at the mountain of papers. "We're well above budget this year, what with the failed rocket that had to be written off and the extra costs of the all of the additional reindeer test runs. We may as well incorporate ourselves. Santa Claus dot-com."

Santa gazed at her with a sad look. "It's too much for me. I can't help but think about retiring."

Mrs. Claus put her fork down.

"Maybe you should try to remember the old days, when things were simpler," she said, "before the demographics reports and budgets buried you in computer printouts."

Santa put his papers down. His wife's soft voice always gave him comfort. The soft touch of her hand on his did, too.

"Remember your original first love of giving gifts to the poor children?"

Santa knew she was right, of course. There had been an original reason from long, long ago, back when he was still young and searching to discover his true purpose in life. Long ago, but if he thought about it, not really that long ago, after all...

~~~

...Young Bishop Nicholas lit the candles of the stone chapel of Myra in silence, one by one. When he finished with the candelabra on the left side of the sanctuary, he walked across to light the other candelabra. Finished with the second set, he stepped forward to the large table and dipped his candlelighter to the large white vigil pillar candle. Once the flame flared, he blew out the candlelighter, put it down across the table, and knelt in the shadows, the vigil candle casting a warm glow upward to the large crucifix hanging on the wall.

He closed his eyes and as he prayed, he heard

the large front doors part. Footsteps walked up the aisle. Someone knelt down, somewhere in the back of the chapel. It was not unusual for people to come in at various times of the day, and the young bishop continued in private prayer.

"Forgive me, Father," he heard a vaguely-familiar voice whisper. "My business has suffered, and I have failed as a father. I cannot provide for my daughters, and I see no possibilities." The man's voice cracked and he took a slow, deep breath. "I have no dowry for my eldest," the man continued, "and she will have no means to live, except..." The man's voice broke. "...by selling herself."

Bishop Nicholas closed out his silent prayer, bothered by the torment he heard.

"For the young ones, it is only a matter of time. I...I fear for my daughters...." Another quaver slipped through the man's lips and he quietly wept for a moment. "Lord, on this night, I beg of you, hear my plea. Answer my prayer, send us a sign that things might be better, as you did on the night of your Son's birth. Our hope is in you, alone. Amen."

The man rose. Footsteps walked away, and the large door swung closed.

When he had finished his duties, Bishop Nicholas headed out, a heaviness weighing down his heart. Sunset had passed and in the streets, people walked back to their homes, warm breaths floating through the night chill. Tomorrow morning, the Archbishop would lead the Christmas Day Mass for all the townsfolk. Nicholas locked the heavy doors of the chapel and walked through town, greeting people along the way.

On the outskirts of town, he passed a house where three young sisters hurriedly washed their laundry. He knew their names were Dora, Helen, and Pauline, the daughters of old Demitri, a maritime merchant who had tragically lost half of his ships in a devastating storm on the Mediterranean, four months ago, and had struggled to recover, since.

Nicholas paused.

He knew that Dora was sixteen, Helen was thirteen, and Pauline was ten, and that their mother had fallen into a well and died, many years ago. Though he didn't lay eyes on the man who had come to the chapel, earlier, he knew that the voice belonged to Demitri.

Finished, the girls went inside their house. Nicholas could see through the window that they hung their clean laundry over the fireplace to dry, below the family crucifix.

After walking through the town, Nicholas returned to the chapel and his adjoining apartment. Still agitated, he didn't eat or sleep at all, that night. Instead, he prayed for hours in solitude and darkness. Sometime deep into the night, he seemed to fall into a trance and a light appeared before him for several minutes. It was a light that didn't hurt his eyes, though it was blindingly bright, and it spoke to him in a gentle but clear voice. He nodded his head, and the light faded away. Finally, after another hour of prayer, he got up, dressed in his red robe, and walked over to the chapel.

He descended the stone steps to the underground vault and brought forth three small solid gold balls. His parents had given these to him when he was a small child, but he quickly realized that he would never need the money. His childhood had been rich in the affluence of his father's successful business ventures. So as he entered adulthood and the ministry, he kept them handy, waiting for someone who would need them. He gazed at them, one last time, and he knew these glittering tokens finally had a purpose. Pocketing them, he went outside to the back, where his white horse stood. He mounted it and rode quickly, but quietly, back to Demitri's house.

When he arrived, he directed the horse over to the lowest point of the rooftop eaves. Standing on the horse, he climbed up on the roof and wiggled his way down the chimney and into the house. The fireplace was still hot, but he was able to reach over and tuck the gold balls into three of the stockings that hung over the hearth. Then he began climbing back up.

"Who's there?"

It was Demitri, apparently hearing the noises of Nicholas crawling up.

When he pulled himself back out of the

chimney, he could hear Demitri unlocking and opening the front door.

"Who's there?"

Nicholas scrambled as quickly as he could down the slippery slope of the roof and back down onto his horse.

"*Bishop 'Cholas?*"

After the horse leaped high over the fence, Nicholas galloped away into the night....

~~~

...The memories of that first night, and his first Christmas Eve presents to three poor young girls, could feel like yesterday if he kept the feeling close to his heart. It had been long ago, and times had changed. But he realized, for all the advancements of modern society, some constants remained. There were still more in need than in excess. He just had to remember the silent children around the world, the poor and hopeless, and the many who nobody paid attention to.

Mrs. Claus nodded. "Yes, dear, it was a special night—and you were special, too. I was very lucky I happened to look out my window and see you from across the alley. Promise me, dear, that you'll never change."

Santa gave her a warm but worn smile. He had changed—grown older and less robust—but his mission hadn't. Not really. "All right dear, I promise."

* * *

Scooter wasn't sure why he was in this oversized office, but he was curious, nevertheless. He stood with Serge while Bjork and Dr. Olaf sat in brown leather chairs before a large, empty desk, waiting. A third chair sat unoccupied. For who, Scooter wasn't sure.

The door opened and Haggen entered. Bjork motioned for Haggen to take the empty seat. Now, Scooter was curious what Haggen's role would be in this meeting.

An unmarked side door opened and Piotr stepped in. "Please rise."

Scooter and Serge were already on their feet, obviously. Bjork, Haggen, and Dr. Olaf stood, and old Tomte, the rotund, undersized Elf Emeritus, slowly shuffled in with his cane, grumbling his annoyance with each labored step. Scooter had never seen the white-haired Tomte in person before, though everyone knew of the ancient one—Santa's original Chief of Staff—whose white beard was so long it dragged on the ground.

"Please be seated," Tomte croaked. He stepped behind the desk and lowered himself into his black, high-backed chair. He placed his spectacles on his nose as Bjork handed him the final report. After skimming through the contents, Tomte put the report down and took off his spectacles. "Well, this is all very good, gentlemen. Excellent work."

"Thank you, your excellency." Bjork bowed. Scooter followed suit when he saw Serge also bow.

Tomte then parted his beard and took a piece of paper out of his pocket. "I have a note from Santa Claus. It reads, 'I am pleased with the outstanding work of the engineering department, this year. The new sleigh initiative has produced an improved vehicle which should be of great help to me. I look forward to sharing this year's trip with a member of Bjork's staff. Yours, C.'"

Tomte re-pocketed the paper, let out a deep breath, and smiled, deep wrinkles crinkling his face.

Scooter glanced around, unsure of what was next. Haggen fidgeted in his seat.

"Bjork, who have you chosen to pilot the inaugural sleigh ride?"

Bjork hesitated. He cleared his throat and stepped forward.

Tomte's smile melted away. "Eh?" He raised one of his bushy white eyebrows. "Is there an issue, Bjork?"

"Ah," Bjork began, "just among my staff, there is more than one worthy candidate, everyone who is here with me today. Serge is my best pilot and he had performed the majority of the test flights. Under normal circumstances, he would most assuredly be my selection, with young Scooter as his backup. However, Scooter has called to our attention some special circumstances. Haggen, the chief herdsman, has correctly pointed out that we have not taken into account any special accommodations for the reindeer flying in turbulence in our new design.

Unfortunately, it is too late to make any design changes so they will be unprotected, as usual."

Now Scooter understood. After that night at the Blue Ice tavern, he had tried to implement some of Haggen's half-drunken ramblings. Scooter thought they actually made sense, but he simply didn't have enough time to bring anything to fruition. So he went to Serge and Bjork with what he felt was the best—though radical—idea, hoping that he knew Serge well enough to assume that he wouldn't be offended. Fortunately, Serge wasn't.

"As a major responsibility will be to monitor the well-being of the reindeer," Bjork continued, "we feel it best to recommend Haggen to be the elf assistant. He has the best experience for that."

Tomte crossed his arms. "Hmmm. Interesting." With eyebrows furled and his black eyes now emitting a piercing, penetrating stare, he turned to Haggen. "You are not a pilot, are you?"

Haggen shook his head. "No, sir."

"Nor were you involved in the building of the sleigh?"

He shifted in his seat, clearly uncomfortable. "No, sir."

"Have you been well-trained to handle the sleigh in poor weather?"

Feeling sorry for Haggen, Scooter stepped in to help. "Excellency, Haggen is technically solid." He paused when Tomte swung his gaze onto him, but decided to plow ahead. "We have full confidence in the new sleigh, and in him."

"Yes," Bjork added.

Tomte looked at Haggen, again. He wrinkled his nose, took a deep breath, then finally nodded. "Very well, then." He addressed Bjork. "I will trust that you know what's best."

"Thank you, sir," Haggen said, a noticeable relief in his voice. He turned to face the engineers. "Thank you, all."

Scooter smiled.

Out of the corner of his eye, Haggen spied Helga leading little Holly into the hangar to watch. Many of the other young reindeer peered in through the door. Members of the different elf staffs milled about the sleigh, working. The toy department was loading the last of the gifts and testing the computer, and Scooter and the engineers were making final adjustments on the now-glowing power core while Haggen ran through the checklist from his sidecar.

The weather reports hadn't changed. Storm systems from the lower latitudes had made their way north, covering the polar regions in wind, snow, and lightning. Everybody had agreed to take no chances. In the middle of the loading area, harnessed to the large sleigh, stood the "A" team: Dasher, Dancer, Prancer, Vixen, Comet, and Cupid, with Rudolph in front. Donner was tied to Santa's landing car, while Blitzen would pull Haggen's sidecar.

"Haggen!"

Haggen turned to see Scooter approach, his arm waving. Scooter held a large stack of what looked to be thermal blankets.

"I think these will help," Scooter said. "There's still enough time to put these on."

Haggen jumped down. "Thanks, Scooter."

He took half of the stack and together, they draped the heavy blankets over the reindeer, tying them securely around their necks and bodies.

"Where did you find these?" Haggen asked when they were done.

Scooter shrugged his shoulders. "I don't know."

"Huh?" The answer sounded too innocent to avoid suspicion. Haggen hoped that Scooter hadn't lifted them from the toymakers' dormitory.

Scooter looked at Haggen. "Okay, I made them last night. The sleigh was done, so I had some spare time."

"You made them?"

Now Haggen looked at Scooter, fleeting thoughts—and reconsiderations—passing through his mind. Scooter worked quietly, rarely drawing attention to himself, and rarely earning recognition.

"Are we ready, Haggen?" asked Santa Claus, entering the hangar in full, red-robed uniform.

"Uh, yes...." Haggen answered, turning around.

"Let's be on our way, then."

Santa gave Mrs. Claus his traditional kiss, climbed into his luxuriously-comfortable chair, and buckled his seat-belt. Haggen, likewise, climbed into his sidecar and zeroed the GPS location grid. Then, he paused again, the same thoughts and reconsiderations stubbornly clinging to his mind. He looked at Holly, standing with Helga, took a deep sigh, and slowly climbed out.

"Santa," he said, "you need someone who is equally good at piloting the sleigh and watching out for the reindeer." A wave of sadness swept over him, but he knew he was doing the right thing. "That's not me. Scooter should be flying with you."

"Sir?" Scooter asked, surprised.

"Don't you agree, Santa?" Haggen asked. "You know everyone best."

Santa nodded, smiling sympathetically. "Yes, I have noticed. That's very selfless of you, Haggen. I know how you must worry about the reindeer."

"My place is with my herd." Haggen stepped away to join Holly and the rest of the reindeer.

"Don't worry, Haggen, we'll take good care of them," Santa said. "Won't we, Master Scooter?"

Haggen glanced down at little Holly, then over at Scooter, both members of the next generation, and he let out a sad but strangely proud sigh.

Serge gave an uncertain Scooter a quick pat on the back. "Yes, sir," Scooter answered, "we will." After receiving a firm handshake from Bjork, Scooter stepped forward and climbed into the sidecar, where Haggen had just vacated. He gave the instruments a quick check and said, "All systems ready, sir."

"Here we go," Bjork said, rubbing his hands. Turning forward, he called out, "Open the hangar doors."

Haggen watched four of his mighty off-duty reindeer pull open the massive stone gates, revealing a dark and stormy night with the wind howling and the snow swirling over the faraway mountaintops. A flash of lightning momentarily lit up the heavens and the blast of chilled air invaded the hangar bay.

"Running light on," Santa called out.

Rudolph nodded and his red nose intensified into a sharp beacon that cut into the vortex of the night.

"Releasing the emergency brake," Scooter reported.

"Ahead, one quarter impulse," Santa ordered.

"One quarter impulse," echoed Scooter, "aye." He eased the throttle forward.

The team charged ahead, rumbling down the flight deck, the sleigh roaring to life behind them, the power core in the tail intensifying into a luminous blue-white glow. They reached the end of the bay and Rudolph launched himself into the air, followed by the others, as they had done countless times in the past. Donner and Blitzen leaped high and pulled with all their strength and the three-car sleigh, *North Star One*, went airborne, to the cheers of the crowd.

Haggen bent down and cradled young Holly in his arms. The *Santamobile*. It was a magnificent sight.

"Look," he said to her, pointing out the red light that rose higher and higher, "Look and be proud of your magnificent mother and father, little child. Someday, you'll be joining them too, and you'll see all the children of the world, of every race, belief, and yes, behavior, good and bad. Some things will never change, and Santa will visit every one of them."

"Come in, *North Star One*."

Scooter picked up the receiver. "*North Star One*, from high above the Arctic Ocean."

"How are you doing up there?" Serge asked, over the speaker.

Scooter checked his instruments. "We're about 500 feet above the storm clouds, not high enough to need the oxygen tanks, yet. But high enough to admire the view."

"View? Of what? The storm, below?"

Scooter marveled at the rainbow of colors swirling all about him. "No. The Aurora. You should see it, Serge. It's so much better up close in person than in the pictures. I can't even describe how it dances to its own rhythm."

"Please don't rub it in. How is Santa doing?"

Scooter smiled. "He's finishing up his first fruit snack, now. And please tell Haggen the reindeer are finishing their first snack, as well."

"He's right here, listening."

"Oh, good," Scooter said, trying to keep his excitement in check. "I've got good news. I checked the contingent inventory on the computer and found extra football helmets. While we've been cruising, I managed to punch antler holes in them so the reindeer can wear them, if they need to."

There was a brief pause, then the sound of laughter from Serge and Haggen.

A soft beep sounded from the dashboard, grabbing Scooter's attention. "Approaching our first stop, Santa."

"Okay, Master Scooter, time to put the snacks away."

"And the helmets on."

Scooter operated the robotic arm, manually. It slid back and forth with a soft whine, ferrying deer feed back to the feed tank and bringing the helmets out to the reindeer. After retracting the robot arm, Scooter flipped the convertible top switch. "Tops coming up." Now, he would see if this new sleigh would be worth replacing the old, sentimental classic.

"Here we go," Santa said. "Into the maelstrom...."

The storms buffeted the sleigh even worse than the year before. With both Santa and Scooter covered by their convertible tops, they were now relying solely on their instruments for navigation. Earlier, in addition to the helmets, Scooter had found nine excess pair of ski goggles, which he quickly put over the reindeer, also using the handy-dandy, multi-functional robotic feed arm. The weather station had managed to locate a narrow seam between storm centers that they could ride along. They would still take the atmospheric pounding, but avoid the worst of it.

"Santa," Scooter said into the intercom. He didn't want to sound too much like a young fanboy, but he couldn't help himself. This might be the closest he would ever get to building Santa his modern sleigh. If anything failed on the ride, and they didn't make it back, he wanted Santa to know how he felt. "I just wanted to say what a privilege it is to ride with you, sir."

"Master Scooter, it's my privilege to share this journey with you. Thank you for all your work. You're a credit to your generation."

Scooter felt like the young elf receiving the toy sleigh from Santa, again. Only this time, it was the real thing. For a second, he couldn't help but wonder how he got so lucky, building and flying Santa's 21st century sleigh. But only for a second, as the sleigh suffered a major jolt from the turbulence.

On the GPS, the marker for the first town in Siberia lit up. Seeing this, Scooter eased the steering gear forward. "Beginning descent."

They plunged through the cloud layers, the sleigh rocking back and forth from the wind, sleet, and hail. A particularly violent shake would have knocked Scooter out of his seat, if it weren't for his seat belt. The deluge of clang-clangs against the top told him that large hailstones were bombarding the sleigh, just as he had feared. A loud thunderclap echoed throughout the vessel. Scooter could feel his fear threatening to engulf him.

"Santa?" he quickly called into the intercom.

"Yes, Master Scooter?"

He had to focus on the job—Santa's safety. "Are you doing okay, sir?"

Another jolt rocked the sleigh.

"I'm holding up. Are you handling things all right?"

Scooter's stomach was queasy. "We're on instrument control." He felt like throwing up. "It shouldn't be much longer." I hope.

The sleigh dropped—and Scooter suddenly had images of The End. But before he knew it, the vessel righted itself, again. He took a deep breath. Not much longer.

Just like that, the rocking stopped and a gentle sway came over the sleigh. Scooter, realizing that he was drenched in a cold sweat, quickly re-focused on the job and checked his altimeter. "I think we're through, sir."

A burst of static broke over the comm speaker and then it cleared and Serge's voice came through, saying, "Come in, *North Star One*. We've picked you up on our tracking screen. Do you read? Over."

Scooter grabbed the receiver and hurriedly said, "This is *North Star One*, still in one piece." He took a deep breath and steadied his trembling hand. "Santa?"

A pause. "I'm okay, Scooter."

Scooter took another deep breath. "I think we're through the clouds. Please stand by while we open the top."

He flipped the two toggle switches on the dashboard and the convertible tops slowly slid open, away, and down, revealing a steady but gentle snowfall all around them. Ahead were the reindeer, still going strong. In the distance, at the base of a snow-capped mountain range, sat the darkened houses of a tiny Northern village, approaching rapidly. Next to him, a safe and sound Santa gave Scooter a smile and a thumbs up.

"We made it!" Scooter exclaimed, his heart racing with excitement. He flipped up two tiny switches, arming the latches of the landing car. "Now preparing the lander for departure." When the lights on the panel all turned green, he turned to Santa and said, "Ready, sir."

"Thank you, Master Scooter." Santa took the roster printout from the computer, tucked it into the pocket of his red fur coat, unfastened his seat belt, climbed from his chair into the lander, and fastened the seat belt.

"Ready, Donner?" asked Santa. "Let's get Christmas started." He gave Scooter his signature chortle. "Ho-ho-ho...Here we go!"

Smiling, Scooter flipped the two switches down, releasing Santa's lander. Once the lander had cleared away, Scooter pulled the sleigh up into a circular holding pattern, high above the Siberian village, and took out his pocket camera.

Below, Santa's lander followed Donner down through the gentle snowfall, gliding toward the rooftops, its rear trunk packed full of bags of toys and gifts for the sleeping children. Scooter snapped the picture and transferred it to his view screen. After returning to the castle, some twenty-four hours from now, he would ask the gift staff to memorialize the picture into a small plaque, his own personal memento from this special ride, the maiden voyage of Santa's new sleigh, the *North Star One*.

The End

About the author:

After a successful 25-year career in the utility industry, Moses Solomon set sail on a new career journey as a science fiction/fantasy writer. The ebook edition of *The Santamobile*, a tale of Santa Claus in the 21st century, received the following words of praise:

"...even readers not into fantasy will enjoy this nice short Christmas story."

"What can I say? This is a really well put-together book that everyone preteen and up should read..."

Moses Solomon is also the author of two new science fiction novellas, both set in the Euranian star cluster. *The Terror of Mapooly* introduces the spacefaring Euranians at the end of the Galactic Revolutions.

The Euranian setting is revisited in *Timegazer*, which takes place fifty years later.

Follow Moses Solomon's tales of Eurania at **http://eurania.wordpress.com/** and on Twitter (**@MoSolomon299**).

www.ingramcontent.com/pod-product-compliance
Lightning Source LLC
Chambersburg PA
CBHW020143150626
46552CB00021B/1432